O

Published in the United States of America by The Child's World®
1980 Lookout Drive • Mankato, MN 56003-1705
800-599-READ • www.childsworld.com

ACKNOWLEDGMENTS
The Child's World®: Mary Berendes, Publishing Director
The Design Lab: Kathleen Petelinsek, Design and Page Production
Literacy Consultants: Cecilia Minden, PhD, and Joanne Meier, PhD

LIBRARY OF CONGRESS
CATALOGING-IN-PUBLICATION DATA
Moncure, Jane Belk.
  My "o" sound box / by Jane Belk Moncure ; illustrated
by Rebecca Thornburgh.
     p. cm. — (Sound box books)
  Summary: "Little o has an adventure with items beginning with
his letter's sound, such as an ox, an ostrich, an octopus, and
otters."—Provided by publisher.
  ISBN 978-1-60253-155-0 (library bound : alk. paper)
  [1. Alphabet.] I. Thornburgh, Rebecca McKillip, ill. II. Title.
III. Series.
  PZ7.M739Myo 2009
  [E]—dc22   2008033171

A NOTE TO PARENTS AND EDUCATORS:

Magic moon machines and five fat frogs are just a few of the fun things you can share with children by reading books with them. Reading aloud helps children in so many ways! It introduces them to new words, motivates them to develop their own reading skills, and expands their attention span and listening abilities. So it's important to find time each day to share a book or two . . . or three!

As you read with young children, you can help develop their understanding of how print works by talking about the parts of the book—the cover, the title, the illustrations, and the words that tell the story. As you read, use your finger to point to each word, modeling a gentle sweep from left to right.

Simple word games help develop important prereading skills, including an understanding of rhyme and alliteration (when words share the same beginning sound, such as "six" and "sand"). Try playing with words from a book you've just shared: "What other words start with the same sound as moon?" "Cat and hat, do those words rhyme?" The possibilities are endless—and so are the rewards!

My "o" Sound Box®

(This book uses only the short "o" sound in the story line. Words beginning with the long "o" sound are included at the end of the book.)

O

WRITTEN BY JANE BELK MONCURE

ILLUSTRATED BY REBECCA THORNBURGH

Little  had a box. "I will find things that begin with my **O** sound," he said. "I will put them into my sound box."

Little  hopped along.

Hop! Hop! Hop!

He found otters in a pond.

Did he put the otters into his box?

He did.

Little 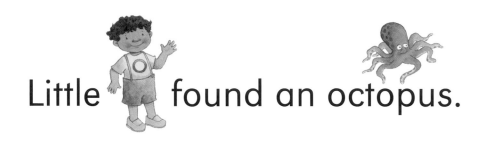 found an octopus.

Did he put the octopus into the  box with the otters? He did.

But the otters did not like

the octopus.

The otters hopped out of the box.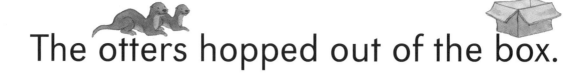

Hop! Hop! Hop!

Little  put a top on the box

so the octopus could not get out.

Then he put the otters on top of

the box.

Away he went. Hop! Hop! Hop!

Then Little  found an ostrich.

He hopped on the ostrich.

"Hop!" he said.

But the ostrich would not hop.

So Little  put the ostrich on

top of the box.

Now the box was heavy.

Little  found an ox.

"You are just what I need for my 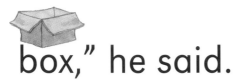 box," he said.

Away they went—Hop! Hop!

Hop!—all the way home.

Little  took his things out of
the box.

What funny things he had!

Little 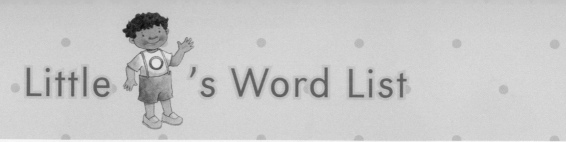's Word List

octopus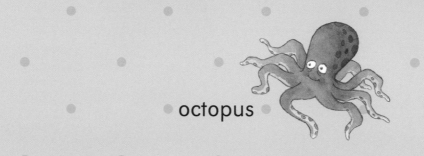

ostrich

otter

ox

28

Other Words with the Short "o" Sound

October
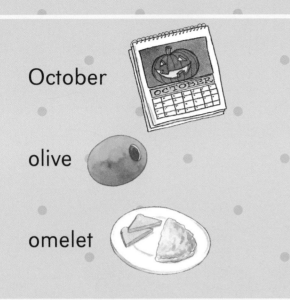

olive

omelet

orange

orangutan

owl

Words with the Long "o" Sound

Little "o" has another sound in some words. He says his name, "o."
Can you read these words? Listen for Little "o's" name.

oar
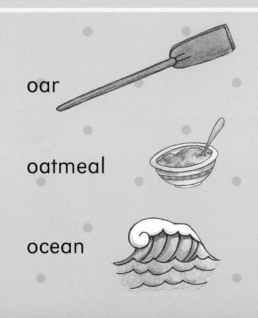

oatmeal

ocean

okra
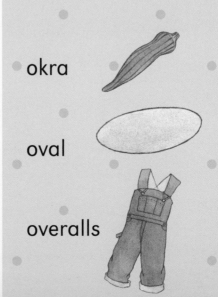

oval

overalls

More to Do!

Little  had a funny group of animals in his box. Do you think otters, octopuses, ostriches, and oxen live in boxes? No, of course not. Each of these animals lives in the home that is best for them. Think about each animal. Where do you think they live?

Directions:

The place in which an animal lives is called its *habitat*. Can you match each animal with the correct habitat description?

A. This cute animal is happy both on land and in the water. You can see it running along riverbanks or floating in the sea.

B. This animal lives on the plains of Africa. It can run very fast. It has long, powerful legs to carry it away from danger.

C. This animal is very large. Its hooves help it move along rough, bumpy areas. It easily moves through grassy fields, too.

D. This animal has eight squiggly arms. It is very shy and likes to hide in ocean caves and cracks.

ostrich

octopus

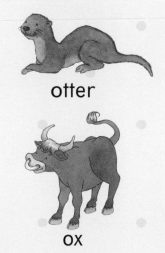

otter

ox

(Answers: A. otter; B. ostrich; C. ox; D. octopus)

About the Author

Best-selling author Jane Belk Moncure has written over 300 books throughout her teaching and writing career. After earning a Master's degree in Early Childhood Education from Columbia University, she became one of the pioneers in that field. In 1956, she helped form the Virginia Association for Early Childhood Education, which established the first statewide standards for teachers of young children.

Inspired by her work in the classroom, Mrs. Moncure's books have become standards in primary education, and her name is recognized across the country. Her success is reflected not only in her books' popularity with parents, children, and educators, but also by numerous awards, including the 1984 C. S. Lewis Gold Medal Award.

About the Illustrator

Rebecca Thornburgh lives in a pleasantly spooky old house in Philadelphia. If she's not at her drawing table, she's reading—or singing with her band, called Reckless Amateurs. Rebecca has one husband, two daughters, and two silly dogs.